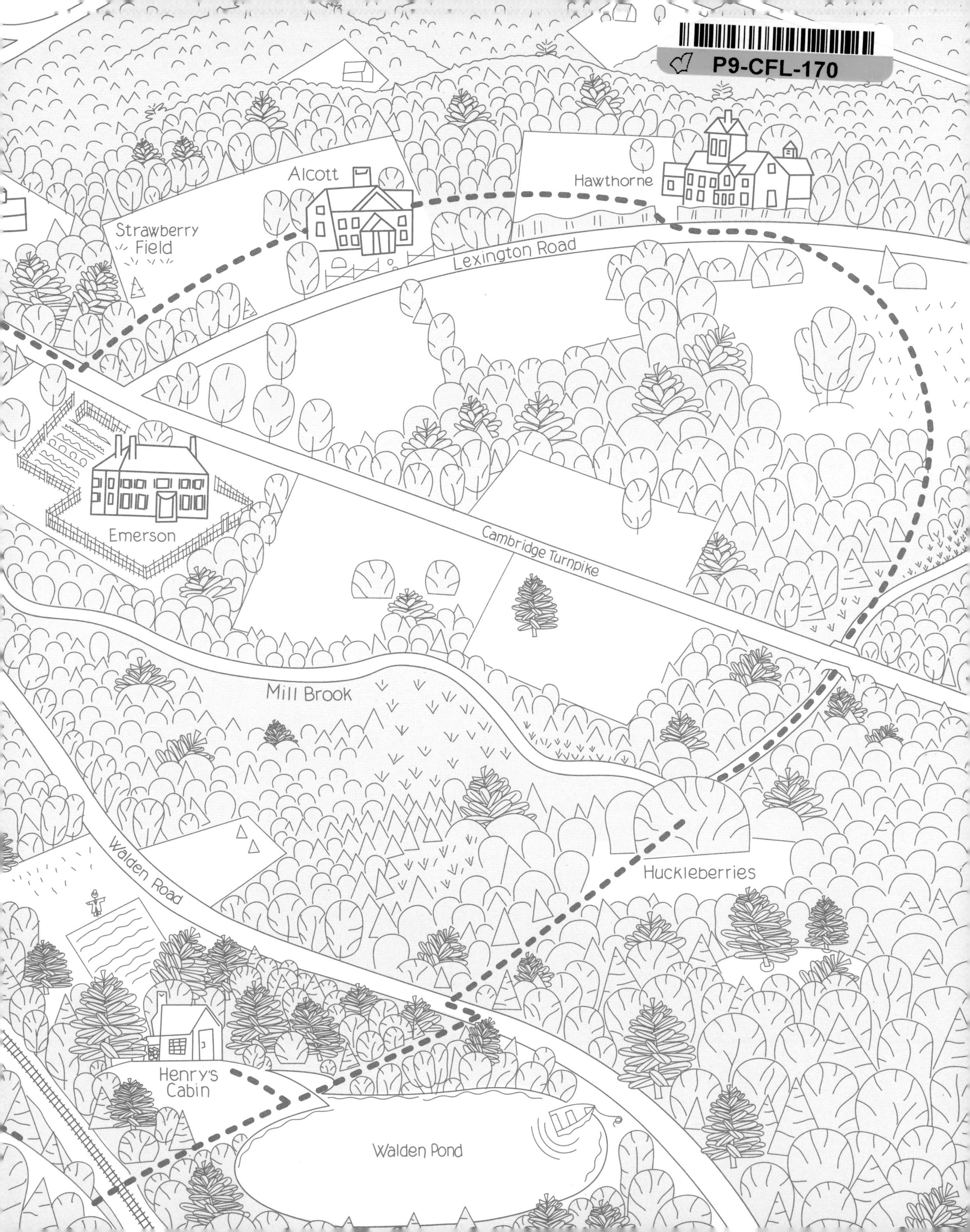
Alcott
Hawthorne
Strawberry Field
Lexington Road
Emerson
Cambridge Turnpike
Mill Brook
Walden Road
Huckleberries
Henry's Cabin
Walden Pond

HENRY WORKS

For Anya, Lise, and Reed

www.houghtonmifflinbooks.com

The text of this book is set in 15-point ITC Century Book.
The illustrations are colored pencil and paint on paper.

Library of Congress Cataloging-in-Publication Data

Johnson, D. B. (Donald B.), 1944–
Henry works / by D. B. Johnson.
p. cm.
Summary: On a misty morning, Henry, a bear modeled after Henry David Thoreau, shows his awareness of nature as he helps neighbors during his walk to work.
ISBN 0-618-42003-7
1. Thoreau, Henry David, 1817–1862—Juvenile fiction. [1. Thoreau, Henry David, 1817–1862—Fiction. 2. Nature—Fiction. 3. Walking—Fiction. 4. Bears—Fiction. 5. Animals—Fiction. 6. Authorship—Fiction.] I. Title.
PZ7.J6316355Hg 2004
[E]—dc22
2003017698

Printed in Singapore
TWP 10 9 8 7 6 5 4 3 2 1

HENRY WORKS

by D. B. Johnson

Houghton Mifflin Company
Boston 2004

It is a misty, mizzling morning. Henry steps out the door and sniffs the air. It is a perfect day to walk to work.

Henry stops beside the pond to dig comfrey root. Channing walks by.

"Henry," he says, "you're not doing anything today—come fishing with me."

"Not today," says Henry. "I'm walking to work." Henry puts the comfrey root in his hat and walks down the path.

From the top of a hill, Henry sees clouds far away. It has been a dry summer, but he knows it will rain today.

The rain will not come until afternoon, so Henry fills his cup with water and sprinkles it on the milkweed flowers. Hosmer meets him on the path.

"Are you being a rain cloud today, Henry?" he asks.

"I'm walking to work," Henry says.

At the brook, Henry cuts a pole from a pine branch. With it he pushes three crossing stones into place. He puts the pine needles in his hat with the comfrey root.

Henry tramps a trail across Hosmer's field and finds a fox's den. Mrs. Hosmer is sitting at her front window. Henry calls to her.

"Keep your chickens inside tonight—there's a fox around," he says. He leaves a branch of sweet-smelling pine on her window ledge.

In town, Henry meets the postmaster.

"Henry," he says, "I can't walk on my sore foot. Since you're not working, can you take this letter to Emerson?"

"I'm walking to work right now," Henry says, "but I'll take it to him on my way." Henry takes the comfrey root out of his hat and gives it to the postmaster. It will make his foot better.

Henry finds Emerson in his garden and gives him the letter.

Emerson says, “The woodchucks are eating everything in my garden, Henry!”

“I can take care of the woodchucks,” says Henry. “I’ll bring them out to the country on my way to work.” Henry plays his flute and the woodchucks run to him. He tucks one in each pocket and walks off through the woods.

In Alcott's field, where Henry sets the woodchucks free, he finds a patch of wild strawberries. He digs up some of the plants and puts them in his hat. Mrs. Alcott is hanging shirts to dry in the yard.

"You'll have to bring in those shirts soon," Henry tells her. "It's going to rain in an hour."

Henry walks along the road to Hawthorne's house. Inside the fence, the garden is growing wild with grapes and raspberries. Henry takes the strawberry plants out of his hat and finds a perfect place for them in Mrs. Hawthorne's garden.

It starts to rain. Henry walks in the mill brook, measuring the shallow water as he goes. Soon he meets Old Flint sitting on the bank.

"Are you taking a bath, Henry?" asks Flint.

"No," says Henry, "I'm just walking to work."

Henry climbs out of the brook and into the middle of a big huckleberry bush. He crawls under it to cut away the tangles and picks berries until his pockets are full. Henry marks a path from the road to the huckleberry bush.

As Henry walks down the path to his cabin, he meets Channing, carrying his fishing pole. He shows Henry the fish he has caught.

"Did you go to work, Henry?" he asks.

"I'm just getting to work now," says Henry.

"What IS your work?" Channing asks.

"It's writing," says Henry. "I'm writing a book."

Henry turns toward his cabin. All day he has taken care of things in the woods and in town. Now he is back where he started. Inside he lights a fire. He hangs up his hat and coat. Then Henry sits at his desk to begin his book.

"Today," he writes, "I took a walk in the woods."

About Henry's Work

This story is about the real life of Henry David Thoreau. He lived in Concord, Massachusetts, more than 150 years ago. Back then, only a few people went to college. And they usually became preachers, teachers, doctors, or lawyers. After Henry went to Harvard, he did not want to do any of those jobs. He tried teaching, but he did not like to punish the students. He tried working in his father's pencil factory. Even though he invented a better pencil, he was not interested in business.

Henry wanted to go into the woods. He would learn to name birds by their songs and animals by their tracks. He would learn when each flower bloomed. Henry wanted to know the woods as well as any fox or bird knew it. And he wanted to write it all down. Nature, he thought, would teach him how to live a better life. His friend Ralph Waldo Emerson was writing about this very thing. So Emerson helped Henry become a writer. He lent him books and invited him to meet other writers. And he told him to write every day.

Henry was free to write all winter and most of every summer. He worked at jobs just six weeks each year. He fixed people's houses and measured their land. In this way he earned enough money to grow his own food and keep his clothes patched. Henry's neighbors shook their heads. Why was he wasting his life walking in the woods? They could not see the real work Henry was doing.

The story of Henry's walks in the fields and woods grew to seven thousand pages. From those pages came *Walden*, his greatest book.

"For many years I was self-appointed inspector of snow-storms and rain-storms, and did my duty faithfully; surveyor, if not of highways, then of forest paths and all across-lot routes, keeping them open, and ravines bridged and passable at all seasons, where the public heel had testified to their utility.

I have looked after the wild stock of the town, which give a faithful herdsman a good deal of trouble by leaping fences; and I have had an eye to the unfrequented nooks and corners of the farm . . . I have watered the red huckleberry, the sand cherry and the nettle-tree, the red pine and the black ash, the white grape and the yellow violet, which might have withered else in dry seasons."